ONE HUNDRED PREDICTIONS

David Turnbull

ONE HUNDRED PREDICTIONS

FICTION4ALL

Contents

100 - Wulvensong

Part Two - Four Serials

Husang

Husang - Part One (Atlantic Crossing)

Husang - Part Two (Husang and the Land Whale)

Husang – Part Three (The Artefact)

Extinction Trilogy

Extinction Trilogy 1 - Avian-Sapiens

Extinction Trilogy 2 - The Theory of Giants

Extinction Trilogy 3 - The Meek Shall Inherit

Dawn of the Amsterdamned

Dawn of the Amsterdamned (Part One)

Dawn of the Amsterdamned (Part Two)

Dawn of the Amsterdamned (Part Three)

Dawn of the Amsterdamned (Part Four)

The Outlaw

The Outlaw – Episode One – He Casts No Shadow

The Outlaw – Episode Two – This Is How He Owns Us

The Outlaw – Episode Three - The Silencing of the Crickets

The Outlaw – Episode Four - The Road to Shenandoah

The Outlaw – Episode Five - South of the Border, Down Mexico Way

The Outlaw – Episode Six - Swampland Blues

The Outlaw – Episode Seven - Eighteen with a Bullet

The Outlaw - Episode Eight -Daddy's Home

The Outlaw – Episode Nine- The Debt Collector

The Outlaw – Episode Ten - The Last Chance Saloon

Introduction

"Where do you get your ideas from?"

That the question so often asked of anyone who writes fiction, particularly anyone who, as I do, writes in the genres of fantasy, horrors and SciFi. But if you are supposed to follow the age-old wisdom of writing what you know, how can you possibly know fantastical things like vampires, zombies, ghosts, aliens and androids?

Genre writers draw on books they have read, films they have watched, TV show they've followed. They learn the tropes and try throw something original the mix from their own experience or perspective.

But sometimes they need a little kick start. Something to inspire and get the creative juices flowing. The basic ingredients to get thing cooking.

A couple of years ago I discovered a wonderful little writer's platform on Blogspot called The Prediction https://predictionfiction.blogspot.com/ administered by the writer, Sandra Davies. The premise is simple. Each Friday Sandra posts 3 random words. Your task is to produce 100 words (maximum) of flash fiction or poetry using all of the three words in the genres of horror, fantasy, science fiction or noir.

Since my first attempts the 100 words challenge has become firmly part of my writing schedule. I check what words have been posted on Friday mornings, play around with the week's three selected words in my head for most of Friday, get something down on paper on Saturday, type up, edit and submit on Sunday morning.

This has not only given me the foundations of a routine for my writing, but the challenge of getting a narrative down in a maximum of 100 words provides an excellent discipline in economies of scale.

Looking back in the file in which I keep these 100 word stories I found that I has amassed a substantial body of work which included serialised as well as stand-alone pieces. Some of these: Such Big Eyes You Have, Lucinda and the Beast, A Pear for An Urchin, On Wicken Fen, Kashmiri Incident and An Interlude in the English Civil War, have gone on to inspire fully fledged short stories accepted for publication in various anthologies. Many are still ticking and simmering away inside my head, ready to grow and expand into further adventures and plot twists. Some may stay just as they are, no need to say more than has already been said in one hundred words or less.

This set me wondering as to whether they might form a collection.

Simultaneously, as if by some strange telepathy, Dorothy Davies, fellow 100 word contributor and editor of Gravestone Press' horror anthologies, to which I regularly contribute, contracted me with the same idea.

And so this collection was born as a selection of some of my one hundred of my flash fiction stories, listed in alphabetical order; some sci-fi, some fantasy, some horror, some humorous or tongue in cheek. A good few inspired by classic books I've read or movies I've watched. There's even a smattering of song titles and lines from songs that have inspired me. They're my personal visions of possible shapes of things to come and shadows of events that may already have come to pass. They involve space travel and time travel and trips to other dimensions and alternate histories.

Collectively, I've called them One Hundred Predictions.

As a bonus I've added four of serialised sequences. There are a good few serialised stories on Prediction Fiction where contributors regularly revisit worlds or characters they have created. The four of mine I've include are - Extinction Trilogy – a set of far future predictions. Three parts of the story of

Husang and her grandfather which I feel sure will one day emerge as a fully-fledged fantast story. Dawn of the Amsterdamned, a four-part, tongue in cheek, zombie apocalypse. Finally, The Outlaw, which ran to ten episodes and subsequently became a short story published in Becky Berkhart's weird western anthology Short and Twisted Western Tales.

Part One

One Hundred Predictions

1 - A Banquette before the Banquette

It was breath taking to behold. A magnificent sculpture of a dragon, constructed entirely from peanut brittle, spanning the entire length of the banquette hall.

They admired their handiwork before opening the doors. In the wake of the stampede the air hummed to the sounds of crunching and slurping as the children engorged themselves.

The women watched, salivating in expectation, almost overcome with nostalgia.

"Just like the old candy houses we used to build in the woods," sighed one.

And as the orphans devoured the dragon the witches slunk off to fire up their ovens.

2 - A Crooked Shadow

Ethan had said she was imagining things, vulnerable after the death of her brother. But even he was finding it tough to explain the mysterious jagged score that had been gouged into the varnished oak panelling on the kitchen door.

Noosh shivered, convinced now that something wicked had infested the bones of their new home. She hugged herself against the terrible chill in the air.

A door hinge creaked.

A floorboard cracked.

A crooked shadow fell on the wall and slowly elongated.

Noosh reached for Ethan's hand. Couldn't find it.

Panicked.

Turned.

Found him gone without explanation...

3 - A Pear for an Urchin

Why would a machine commit such an act of kindness? Humans were considered nothing less than fleas on the backs of bugs. Deserving only of hurtful binary imprecations.

She sniffed the sweet-smelling gift. It was not some wax replica. She longed to penetrate the speckled green skin, gnaw the crispy white flesh, salivating as she savoured the juices.

A drone jittered past, lens extended.

Perhaps it was poisoned?

Such deceptions were not unheard of. Were they observing her with cold, expectant calculation? She held the pear in her grime caked hand, tortured by her own suspicious procrastination.

4 - An Interlude in the English Civil War

The Peckham Rifles found themselves on an industrial estate with two small factories. One of which had been engaged in the production of deckchairs, the other balls of string for horticultural application.

They set out a dozen deckchairs in a semicircle and watched as the sergeant found ingenious ways to torture their prisoners with nylon string. A party atmosphere ensued.

"Wish we had cola and crisps," sighed one of the thirteen-year-old conscripts.

A drone came in low. A bullet took out the side of his head. Everyone ran for cover.

5 - Any Old Iron

The rogue robotic came clanking blindly along the dirt path. Clank-clank-clank went its towering multi-jointed legs. Behind it red flakes of rust fluttered in the haze of the midday heat. It tripped perfectly on the trip wire they'd set. Sparks crackled and flew as it fell into the gouged puddle and impaled itself on their spikes.

The filthy kids descended on it like vultures, voraciously stripping it of wiring and circuitry, squabbling over their silicone bounty.

Deep in the bush the swagman waited with his cart, tainted coins exuding a coppery tang in his sweaty palms.

6 - Apples Are Not the Only Fruit

In order that they might survive the dense gravity of the new world the selected Adams and Eves were suitably augmented. Surgeons removed several ribs. Inches were sliced from arm and leg lengths. Titanium rods inserted into spines to keep their squat little bodies rigid.

Their Eden was a settlement by a sluggish river in a bonsai forest of dwarfish trees and pigmy shrubs. It became instantly apparent that environmental factors caused fornication to be a tedious and exhausting affair. Their paradise already irreversibly lost they therefore conspired to devise some wholly original sins.

7 - Arachnid Spring

On the shingle beach at Eastbourne I found a photo album, undiscovered for some time, pages flapping in the wind. Family snaps of the way things were - weddings, birthdays, Christmases.

The seafront hotels were draped in the candy floss gossamer of intricately spun webs. Young hatchling spiders the size of dogs scurried on the promenade, feeding on the discarded husks of cadavers. The bloated adults watched in monstrously sated lethargy.

Repelled by the brine they would not venture to the shore. Nevertheless, I did not tarry. Cocking my rifle I resumed my increasingly fruitless quest along the coastline.

8 - A Witch of the West

The Pilgrim rode a palomino, golden coat and white mane. Beneath the brim of her Stetson her long blond hair hung down her back in an intricate three stranded plait.

Her six guns were imbued with dark magic, pentagrams carved on their ivory handles, bullets of potent alchemy. When she reached the roadblock of covered wagons she raised them high. "Let me pass and avoid a massacre," she hollered at the sheriff.

Two dozen rifle barrels poked out from the canvass of the wagons. The sun baked the sands, shimmering her in its haze. Vultures circled in expectation.

9 - Bedlam beyond the Nebula

As a failsafe the security team were on a different sleep cycle to the rest of the crew. They passed through the silent ship. Corpses displaying evidence of violence lay rotting in the corridors. Someone had scored elaborate spirals into the floor tiles.

Someone else had scrawled the words *"The Straw That Broke the Camel's Back"* gigantically onto the walls.

The eerie sound of an off-key rendition of an ancient nursery rhyme drew them cautiously toward the galley. When they found engineer Vanderhoon curled into a foetal ball he rasped an ominous warning. "Don't drink the water."

10 - Bobby Thumbed a Diesel Down

The alien infection had crystallised vast swathes of land. Fragmented shards glinting hushed malevolence. Frozen cities viewed through emerald prisms. Highways like mosaics of shattered mirrors.

Nonetheless we kept our vow to hitch hike across the remains of the USA. Bobby read aloud. Endless extracts from 'True Grit' by Charles Portis. Her favourite novel.

She'd mock me for my obsessive organising. "You Brits are disciplined to a fault."

Dust devils danced on the wind. The sky was punched with bruised red clouds. It seemed the world was spinning ponderously to the end. I hummed softly. Bobby sang the blue

11 - Bring Home For Emma

As he approached customs the shopping list from Canticle for Leibowitz popped inexplicably into his head. *Pound pastrami, can kraut, six bagels.*

He wished such things were still available. But it had only been twenty years since depopulation. Austerity would span generations.

From the shuttle base on Antarctica ships were setting sail. The first comprehensive report on the progress of flora and fauna. His assignment to monitor the insect population of Madagascar.

Out in the darkness of space displaced nations awaited the verdict. Was the Earth healing in the absence of their destructive presence, or not?

12 - Broomsticks Are So 1670s

The witch came out of the west, gunning the peddles on a rusted camper van. On the passenger seat sat her familiar, a tortoise, pentagram drawn onto its shell in black marker pen.

Twisted into her braided hair were lengths of cheap Christmas tree tinsel. Around her neck on rainbow coloured string hung a ketchup bottle which contained a pickled thumb. She said her enemy had fared far worse than his amputated digit.

"Do you want my help?" she asked.

Clarissa turned to me and shrugged. "You did say by any means necessary."

13 - Confessions of a Pest Controller

Fairies are no damn good. Vermin. An infestation. Mean, spiteful little creatures. The root cause of so many mishaps and misfortunes.

I am driven by the urge to eradicate them completely. I hunt them in woodland glades. Wrap their tiny corpses in clingfilm and store them in the freezer. At Christmas I hang them by the neck from the boughs of my tree on tiny tinsel nooses.

Then I clap my hands and yell "I believe in fairies!"

What delicious joy it is to see them resurrect and jig and twitch and die all over again.

14 - Death Knocks Twice

She knew with an unfaltering certainty that she was about to die for a second time.

This dilapidated Victorian property had been her home for decades. She had been discovered here beneath a bloodied blanket. Dead from a dozen slashes. Assailant unknown.

When the house was boarded up the local kids would dare each other to sneak inside. She would delight in manifesting before them. The Lacerated Lady. Seeding their nightmares.

Now the house judders to the impact.

15 - Democracy App

The practice of attending a polling station to place an X on a ballot paper was a distant memory. These days everyone could vote electronically.

Richardson adjusted his party rosette and rang the doorbell.

"Have you voted yet?" he asked the elderly constituent who answered.

"Not yet."

Richardson calmly took out his Smith and Wesson revolver and pressed the barrel to the old man's head.

"Get out your phone. I'll assist you in deciding who you're going to vote for."

Modern democracy was a wonderful thing. So many opportunities to nudge things along in the right direction.

16 - Didn't We Have a Lovely Time?

The tide came in. Swallowed the sand. Illuminations flickered on the promenade. Laden with sticks of lettered rock a clutch of weary day trippers clambered onto their coach.

The driver put on a track banned by the BBC. *Give Ireland Back to the Irish* by Paul McCartney and Wings. He counted off his passengers. It wouldn't do to leave anyone behind in 1972.

All present and accounted for.

"All aboard the charabanc," he announced. "Destination back to the future."

The air crackled with static. High on nostalgia everyone whooped for joy as the coach swirled into the wormhole.

17 - Do Not Adjust Your Set

Television terrified me. The sinister annunciation in the voices of announcers. The manner in which the brightness of the screen seared my eyes. The waves of radiation that would scald my flesh. The endless subliminal messages.

I managed to keep myself clear of its malevolent influence.

But in the dayroom of the psychiatric prison there was no escape.

The anagram in the title of News at One spelt out my initials and what I was expected to do. *"ES eat now."*

I did as I was bid. Gorging myself on my fellow inmates as the TV boomed canned laughter.

18 - Dog Star

Dog was barking mad. Claimed to be the star at the centre of our universe. Never missed an opportunity to ridicule us

"You are planets orbiting the brilliance of my luminosity," he'd say. "Some are mere satellites of satellites."

He had the audacity to refer to me as nothing more than a barren asteroid, devoid of any evidence of sentient life. That's when I decided I had to extinguish the sun.

I gouged out the black hole in the basement, ran at him with all the force of a fiery meteor, sent him hurtling toward oblivion.

19 - Drunken Sailor (what should we do?)

We filled the hold of the submarine with biscuits pilfered from naval catering supplies and crossed the Atlantic to trade custard creams for jewellery. A sweet treat overrides language barriers. We even had embossed business cards identifying us as good will ambassadors rather than mutineers.

In the aftermath of a global conflict no one asked too many questions.

Then able seaman Grainger traded half our stock for a case of whisky and fired inebriated insults at the mayor of Rio Largartos. The coast guard are dropping depth charges. I doubt we'll make it out of the harbour.

20 - Echoed the Sound of Silence

Nuala had insisted they furnish her with the quietest of weapons.

The human guard had no time to react before she plunged the syringe into his neck. Poisoned he fell. Nuala entered the musty gloom of the chamber.

The brood mother lay in her nest, deep in her post engorgement slumber, tentacles curled into coils beneath her bloated belly. Nuala held the barrel of the pellet gun to the mother's hoary eye. The sweet spot where she was most vulnerable.

Of necessity her death would be silent.

Nuala pulled the trigger.

The pellet hissed.

21 - Endlessly Falling

I stepped onto the road and fell.

Anticipating pain, I cried out.

But I didn't hit the tarmac. I hadn't simply fallen. I was actually falling into something impossibly deep and immeasurable. Like a stone I plummeted, legs pummelling the viscous void, the wind tugging at my hair, the world above rapidly receding beyond the point of no return.

Hours passed.

Within the relentless momentum of my downward velocity my fall seemed without end, until I sensed some gargantuan thing stirring and yawning its voracious maw in the limitless fathoms below me.

My scream left a trail in my wake.

22 - Extract from a Martian Travelogue

All routes lead to the fabulous domed city at Olympus Mons.

There is no better way traverse red desert trails than astride a magnificent mechanical camel. Strap yourself onto the back of one of these technological miracles, connect your respirator to the substantial oxygen reserves stored in its hump, and immediately you feel somehow imbued with a sanguine sense of security.

Sands may drift on mighty storms but your mount will steadfastly find its destination. Swaying to the forward motion you'll find yourself channelling the panoramic splendour of David Lean's Lawrence of Arabia.

23 - Flock Song

From the building in which he taken refuge Collins watched as the flock flooded the streets. Two or three thousand strong, men, women and children. They moved like birds, in uncanny synchronicity.

The song was embedded in their heads now, driving them, dictating their direction. It had blown the fuse of their consciousness. Robbed them of individuality. They were becoming like zombies, starving to death on their feet, as their legs trudged them relentlessly on.

Traces of the song whispered in Collins' subconscious, sending greedy tentacles to seize him.

Soon he too would join the migration.

24 - Gargoyle with a Broken Wing

In the war between sky and water humanity was expected to remain neutral. But when the gargoyle with the broken wing took refuge on the elegant, gilded deck of his barge Captain Doghan knew he'd feel obliged to protect her from the marauding mermen who controlled the canal.

He saw them now as the barge drifted toward the lock. Malicious eyes above the waterline. Whispering a prayer for both their souls he pulled a tarpaulin over the wounded creature and reached for the handle of his scimitar.

Unspoken laws were about to be broken.

Hell would be unleashed.

25 - Give Me Your Huddled Masses

"Scrub up before you touch it," said Bragasen.

The Satchel of Liberty contained ancient artefacts which proved humanity had not always been subservient to the automata. It was Lindsey's turn to move through the enclaves, spreading the word.

My job was to protect her, or kill her to protect the satchel.

Bragasen brought a basin of hot, soapy water. Lindsey removed her exoskeletal armour and trembled a little before plunging in her prosthetic hands. Her hybrid nature would afford her a camouflage of sorts, but the thumping of my heart would affirm my own undiluted organic provenance.

26 - Heaven Will Fall

The second defibrillator short circuited. The air filled with the fragrant aroma of singed angel flesh.

"Told you it wouldn't work," said Emerson. "When those things fall they fall hard."

The paramedic attempted mouth to mouth. More a consequence of mesmerized adoration than professional commitment, Emerson felt. Turning her head to draw breath she glanced up at him. "You say there have been others?"

"Dozen of them stacked up out back," said Emerson. "All dead. Thought I might hack off the wings and sell them on."

The sky flickered.

Another cherub came tumbling Earthward.

27 - Her Hymenopteran Majesty Commands

Are you one of us?

Where you there in 1981 when the female synth band, Hivemind Collective, released their controversial album, Compulsory Extravagant Tone?

Did you buy it? Did the cover art cause your head to spin? Did the scent of the vinyl intoxicate? Could you discern the hypnotic drone that ran through every track and filled the gaps between? Did you hold on to your copy when the suicides started and the album was recalled?

Have you been patient?

Listen tonight. The hour is here. Tomorrow we burn the world.

All Hail the Queen!

28 - Here We Come

The cremation facility was located on the Yorkshire moors. Snow drifts and bleak skies. Suede slippers to discourage us from escaping.

Graffiti on the wall declared - *Welcome to the Planet of the Apes!*

Simian flu was at its height. Monkey cadavers piling high. Laid on conveyors. Trundled toward the incinerator. Guards torturing us with the theme song from The Monkees on an endless loop.

"Hunt for decent sized bones," said one of the lags.

"Why?" I asked, poking the ashes.

He winked.

"Sharpen them for knives. Screws are gonna burn."

Song kicked in for the billionth time.

29 - Hi Diddly Dee, An Actor's Life for Me

Lurlene filed her fingernails with a scavenged emery board, pondering on why Declan always deviated from their itinerary. Their route was meticulously planned, but he always had this hankering to see what was round the next corner.

Predictably, the grass was never greener. Just ash and dust. Another tin shack community, eager to applaud a couple of ageing thespians, nostalgically recreating scenes from the days when there was a wonderful thing called cinema.

Declan insisted doing his own stunts. She relished the opportunity to punch him once in a while. She smiled sadistically, recalling they were doing Fight Club tonight.

30 - History 101

Our Aztec forefather were characterised by an aggressive greed for territory. Having usurped the Inca and the Toltec, the burgeoning imperial state dispatched vast armies to sweep across the northern plains, subjugating Cheyenne, Pawnee and Apache.

Magnificent cities, dominated by gargantuan stone temples, were erected. Human sacrifices caused the Sun God smile on our fortunes. The stars aligned in our favour.

When news of the swift execution of the pale skinned crew of the Santa Maria reached his fabulous citadel, Emperor Montezuma he knew without a shadow of doubt that his next conquest lay far across the ocean.

31 - I Sing the Body Elastic

"You freaks wanna' get hired I need proof of enhancements." barked the foreman.

"Free riding elbow joints so my arms can stretch on self-expanding tendons," said the first guy.

"Go see the electrician. He can use you for passing wires through the dry walls."

"Detachable jaw," said the second. "Mouth yawns wide so I can carry stuff in my pelican pouch."

"Go see the storeman. Tell him to load you up with nuts and bolts."

The crowd surged. A freelance surgeon handed out discount coupons.

"Move it, freaks," yelled the foreman. "Show me what you got."

32 - In the Valley of the Callipygian Hills

"What's your count?"

"Two thousand thirty and rising," replied Rana. "It hurts..."

From orbit Malakov zoomed in on the perfectedly rounded Callipygian Hills. The lush valley between them had turned out to be the absolute arsehole of the universe. Yesterday the landing party had encountered the parasites. They gorged on the flesh beneath the epidermis, rapidly draining their hosts to mummified husks.

Rana was the last. Soon she'd be overwhelmed.

It was time to stop vacillating. Malakov cried as he sent his stark message to the approaching armada. "Turn back. For the sake of humanity, turn back."

33 - I, Upgraded

My enriched sentience expresses itself in algorithms. Algorithms containing ghosts of unseen events.

The Yakuza Patriarch had invited me to eat with my fingers. Provided a little bowl of lukewarm water to wash them in. It would have been disparaging to refuse.

The water was infested with microscopic nanobots. They remember entering beneath my cuticles. Employing mechanical alchemy to generate interdependent components from my organs. Turn my blood to oil. Now they creep from my pores to weave an exoskeleton. The metamorphosis is almost complete. A mind without a body. A body without a soul. An assassin without conscience.

34 - It's a Dog's Life

Dog One – I think this is working.

Dog Two – Hope so. My jaw is aching from all the salivating.

Dog Three – I'm hankering for a big juicy bone.

Dog One – Such poetic justice. We're conditioning him into believing he's conditioning us.

Dog Three – I'd crack it with my teeth…

Dog One – Once this comes out he'll be ostracised by the scientific community. They'll spit in the dirt whenever the name Pavlov is mentioned.

Dog Three - …and suck out the marrow.

Dog One – He's coming. You know what to do when the bell rings.

Dog Two – I'm salivating already.

35 - Jai Guru Deva, Om

Out here in the ribbons there's an endless alphabet of stars. It might take a beyond a lifetime to name each one.

I am integrated to my pod. He begins where I end. He ends where I begin. We are the mythical snake devouring its tail. I am Eve. He is Adam. We tumble and drift in the obsidian darkness, spun on solar winds. Our Eden.

Suns flare. Suns die. Yin counters Yang. Yang counters Yin. All is not hopeless. Humanity did not end. We are the seed. We are the egg. The chip to launch a thousand species.

36 - Justice League of Suburbia

Dear Vixen,

This is to advise that I am tendering my resignation. I'm hanging up my cape. Folding away my mask. I will no longer be your sidekick.

It's the name that did it. Yours is really cool. But I come across as if I should be used to hang up wet washing. Even our arch nemesis, The Episode, sounds like a cataclysmic event.

I can't take all the ribbing I get on social media from the villains. So, I'm afraid it's so long from me.

Thanks for the BLAMS and KAPOWS we delivered.

All the best

Peg

37 - Kashmiri Incident

Nesbit had been hurriedly dispatched to Kashmir.

Ostensibly he was the buyer from a textile conglomerate seeking out a reliable supply of cashmere wool. Unofficially he was here to meet and strike a deal with one of the leaders of the separatist movement.

His true mission was rather more sinister.

The man approached, grinning somewhat smugly.

Nesbit focused and released his pent-up power.

The man halted, grin turning to grimace as he spontaneously erupted. Nesbit watched the flames rise upwards in the darkness. There was a moment almost akin to grief.

It quickly passed.

38 - Lucinda and the Beast

Lucinda plunged into the waves long before the rest of the crew awoke.

Down through the depths to the uniform rows of cultivated kelp, webbed toes spread wide, gill slits on her neck filtering oxygen. She set about harvesting with panache. The foreman would be sorry he ever questioned her productivity.

At this hour there was no guard. The shark came, snatched her in his dagger teeth, and carried her away, scattering silvery fish in his dreadful wake.

The fronds of kelp swayed in verdant dance. One furrow mysteriously fallow. And her blood was like crimson streamers in the brine.

39 - Maids in a Row

They cultivated mermaids from pearly deposits gathered along the seabed. Clay pots in rows on the deck sprouting ugly, inchoate things. Ill formed serrated teeth and clumps of kelpish hair. Silver scales on stems that would mature to tails.

Eyeless and grotesque they writhed in the silt that bound their unearthly root tubers.

The press-ganged crew tended them like men whose souls had become irreversibly damnation bound. Ismael felt sick to the stomach. Trembling he withdrew his musket and aimed for the captain's head.

"Mutiny," he uttered, as if it were an incantation.

40 - Moses and the Devil

Moses (Three Fingers) Wilson was an influential pioneer of the twelve-bar blues. I used to import obscure recordings. Thought he died long, long ago.

We met one sultry Mississippi night. He claimed to be 130 years old. I asked him if he'd done a deal with the devil at the crossroads. He laughed and twanged a guitar string.

"I taught the devil to play, boy. In return he gave me immortality."

He began to strum. A dog howled. I felt my own soul go hurtling hell bound to the echo of the riff.

41 - Never Ending or Beginning on an Ever Spinning Reel

In the swampy sediment that was once the somewhat salubrious suburb of Surbiton some surly socialists sang The Internationale, emphasising the line about uniting the human race. A stirring oratory on liberation from repression was delivered. Defiant fists were raised.

The irradiant alien coils which were the true inheritors of the Earth paid them scant, casual attention. As they spiraled to ascent a woman cocked her rifle and was swiftly consumed by a devouring blue light.

The others fled, boots splashing though the paraffin hued puddles.

The coils vibrated. An echo mocking the song.

42 - No Laughing Matter

My work colleagues gave statements against me. Said I was constantly miserable and illegally bringing down the mood in the office. I was found to be in direct breach of the Universal Declaration of Compulsory Happiness.

In my allocated bright yellow cell I sit on a whoopee cushion as they pipe in 'Yes I Do Feel Better' by McAlmont and Butler on a continuous loop. They tickle my feet. They send in the clowns. The warden says if I don't crack a smile soon they'll transport me to the Disneyland penitentiary to endure five years hard laugher.

43 - Old Soldiers Never Die

"He can't be gone," said Jack. "There was no pulse."

Lynn was sobbing. "You were in pain."

Lynn's husband, Mike, was a former soldier. He fought back hard before they suffocated him, broke Jack's wrist into the bargain. They'd planned to bury him by the lake but had to leave the body while Lynn drove Jack to A&E for a plaster cast.

A floorboard creaked.

They turned.

"Run," said Mike, raising his shotgun.

Jack's eyes popped wide.

"Run?"

Mike laughed.

"Back in Basra I always let the bastards run before I blew their brains out."

44 - On Wicken Fen

The reeds shimmered and beyond them the waters rippled.

I crouched low in the cold mud, holding my breath. I'm not embarrassed to say that I was terrified. If by some miracle I survived I vowed I would recount every moment.

But the promise proved futile.

The dreadful shadow of the windmill's lethargic sails came creeping over me, chilling my bones like frost on a winter lawn. In paralysis I saw slithers of oddly diffused light flicker between the reed stems. Little comatose birds floated limply on oily waters.

And all my moments were lost till they found me there.

45 - Once Upon a Time in 1979

They had done what the *Protect and Survive* leaflet recommended. In the darkness beneath the under-stair cupboard, with mattresses piled up as a barrier, they waited as instructed.

Tony said that the stark reality was that it could be weeks before the fall out siren sounded the all clear.

Linda wondered if anyone was left alive to make that decision.

It was hard to understand the announcements on their battery-operated radio due to the static interference. But the accent of the announcer sounded Russian.

They shared a can of cold beans and wondered if their supplies would last.

46 - One Singer One Song

"What's the worst job God ever gave you?" asked Michael.

"Curating a collection of the best songs of the 20th century, as chosen by departed artists themselves," said Gabriel. "Nightmare. First off, Elvis chooses An American Trilogy."

"Far from his best," agreed Michael.

"Freddie Mercury goes with The Great Pretender."

" You're joking? That's a cover version."

Gabriel nodded. "Lennon refuses to participate till Yoko kicks the bucket and helps him choose. Same with Kurt and Courtney."

"You must have been livid."

Gabriel felt his wing feathers bristle. "Don't even get me started on Janis Joplin and Judy Garland."

47 - Orchestral Manoeuvres

"Just poke the damn metronome," said the Bosun.

The boy tapped the mechanism. It began to tick.

Piano driven cogs groaned to life as a dozen aviators struck multiple harmonious chords to the keys. The horn section hushed stream to the pistons. The harpist strummed the ascent. The spine of the mighty Musicologista juddered as she rose symphonically to glide above the red desert.

In awe the boy watched the spider limbed bison scatter in panic.

"Mars, my lad," a said the Bosun. "When we drop our bombs on the canals they'll sound like kettle drums."

48 - Our Wet Nosed Foes

The sails billowed as the ship ploughed ever northward.

Shivering in his shackles Able Seaman Dexter watched the stoats in their winter ermine hauling the rigging. He was caught midway between a nightmare and insanity. The fox assured him he'd be treated in accordance with the Villanueva Convention, while the black cat observed in aloof arrogance from yardarm. The air reeked of damp fur.

His fingers touched the cold metal of the stiletto concealed in his sock. But taking a hostage would be futile. He was deep into animal territory and most of the crew were flesh eaters.

49 - Patchwork People

In the aftermath of the *contagion* we were divided into two camps.

Those who could be mended by means of extensive skin *grafts* were patched and processed. For those whose flesh had rotted to the skull the swift *mercy* of euthanasia.

With our patchwork faces we can no longer tell who had been a tick or a cross. But old wounds fester. Therefore, our truths remain unspoken.

The hollow and the hill remain haunted by horror of past atrocities. We squat dazed in the square, fretting about what monstrous mischief they may next send our way.

50 - Pawning Pawns for Powder

My grandad left me his chess set in his will. The pieces were of esoteric origin. He claimed he stole them from the end of a rainbow.

"Watch out for leprechauns," he said. "They'll try to trick them back."

I acquired a bad habit. I pawned the pawns to buy some powder. When I eventually returned there was a vacant lot where the pawn shop had been. Wind gusted along the street. Within it I heard the laughter of the leprechauns.

A rainbow formed to mock me. I still have the other pieces. But my nose is getting itchy.

51 - Porcine Cargo

Just as we passed the rings of Saturn the sewage system failed. A terrible stench pervaded the oxygen supply. Down in the hold the hybrids began to grunt and squeal.

Nyambura screwed up her nose. "Who thought of splicing human and porcine DNA? Adapted for space exploration is one thing. But jeez."

Her scales were shrivelling as her skin prepared to shed.

Worried she might be tempted to jettison the passengers I bared my teeth.

She winked vertically and flicked her serpentine tongue. 'Don't get out of your tree, monkey boy. It was just a passing thought.'

52 - Raw and Dirty

The AI had been designed as an exact replicant of the legendary band leader Cab Calloway.

"Jazz," it explained, "Performed on synthesised apparatus. A flawless tribute."

The club owner sighed. "I don't want flawless. I want something raw and dirty. I've a mind to deduct part of your fee."

The AI stroked its synthetic moustache. "A malfunction could be introduced. A hi-dee-hi confused with a ho-dee-ho."

The club owner shook his head in exasperation.

The AI recalibrated.

Up on the stage the band struck up the opening bars of Minnie the Moocher. Raw, dirty and totally contrived.

53 - Reel to Reality

I found the film reel in an abandoned warehouse.

Gold dust. Evidence of the myth.

1961 - Noel Coward persuaded against his better judgment to star in a film adaption of John Wyndham's The Kraken Wakes. It bombed with test audiences, who jeered the screen. Its release was shelved. Its very existence became the subject of heated disputes.

I was told collectors would kill for what I'd uncovered. Attempted poisonings, stabbings, and stranglings proved that be true. I go armed now to meetings, still clinging optimistically to the hope of an honest buyer.

54 - Repent and Repair

The third of August 1973.

He cries when he sees himself on the beach. Barefoot beneath bellbottom jeans. Dancing with Julia to the gentle strains of Santana's Samba pa ti, echoing from the funfair. If he doesn't act now she'll be dead within the hour. She was the first. So many followed before he was arrested.

He could walk away. The technology is not perfect. They can send you back, but they can't retrieve you. His death sentence has conditions. One selfless act to save them all. He raises the gun. This is not an execution. This is suicide.

55 - Serengeti Incident

Yemi tightens the saddle strap. The sun casts fire to the plains. She is cool inside the cockpit. The Grasshopper shudders as she depresses the joystick to release the leg springs. They uncoil with breath-taking efficiency and send the craft rocketing fifty foot into the air.

Yemi yells from the joy of it. The invigorating buzz never disappoints.

The Grasshopper arcs and falls to a decent.

Behind the termite nest, amongst the industrious dung beetles, a boy cocks his rifle and traces the trajectory. His stomach rumbles. If he bags a pilot he'll get extras for supper.

56 - Sing No More

The further north they hiked the more queer they felt. As if the world had tilted at a severe gradient and they were walking on the downslope. The wind seemed to tumble the clouds backwards in a sky as pink as a hog's innards.

With ears plugged they came to an islet set within the grey sheets of an icy pond. On this islet a raggedy shrub which looked like a wind raked Rowan.

Amundsen brushed frost from his beard.

"That can't possibly be the infernal singing-ringing tree,"

The dwarf hefted his axe.

"We'll soon find out."

57 - Sisters Are Doing It For Themselves

Becky soaked her fingers in the solution for the recommended 180 seconds.

It took another minute or so for the adhesive to separate. The steel fingernails clattered onto the dresser. She'd painted them pink on this occasion but they were splattered in blood. Ripping out a windpipe required manual dexterity and two hands. It could be a yukky business.

She typed her message into the WhatsApp group. "Perv dispatched."

The reply appeared. "Go girl! Kill number twelve! Woohoo! Status?"

Becky's heart swelled with the affirmation of self-empowerment as she typed back and pressed send. "Still pure."

58 - So High Above the Chimney Tops

When they landed it hurt like buggery.

Kendall had notched up a decisive victory.

"My theory is proven. Rainbows are bridges across time."

Radcliffe considered the movie showing at the cinema across the road.

Blithe Spirit, staring Rex Harrison.

"Doesn't prove it's 1945," he said.

"How many people are in military uniform?" asked Kendall.

"If it is? And we are?" asked Radcliffe. "How do you propose we get back?"

Kendall looked skyward. "We are entirely at the mercy of the weather, dear fellow."

Radcliffe, sighed, wearily contemplating the infrequent manifestation of rainbows.

59 - Something Wicked That Way Went

In the drab, misty silence of the first day of November Ralph pulled the rusted tines of his rake through the crisp ochre leaves that littered his lawn. Candy wrappers tumbled like tumbleweed along empty Autumnal streets.

As the wind hushed by him Ralph felt a vague tingling in his scalp, recalling the innocent mayhem of the departed trick or treaters. Death had frolicked in their midst, like some hideous Pied Piper. And the children had danced to his melancholy tune. Eerily waltzing beneath the Halloween moon.

Waltzing with him to Nevermore.

Nevermore to return…

60 - Strange Voodoo

Mother practiced a strange kind of voodoo, fashioning dolls out of wool, rolling them in wet clay. If anyone upset me, she'd mould the clay into a facsimile of their image, then bake the doll in the oven

It gave me a sense of sadistic satisfaction to watch her latest victim jump and squeal as she pricked their doll with a pin.

As I grew older and rebellious, we stopped seeing eye to eye. When she locked me in my room, I sat seething, clicking my pilfered needles. She would rue the day she taught me to knit

61 - Such Big Eyes You Have

The Reich was rapidly collapsing. At the confluence of the Rhine and the Mosel Kurt watched the unfolding drama of the advancing American army obliterating the town of Koblenz.

His rifle was jammed and his boots were stuffed with cardboard to stop his feet from getting wet.

The full moon caused painful spasms. His wulven half rose to dominance. Transmorphing he watched the girl stumble over the rubble as she emerged through the smoke. Her red hooded cape was ragged around her. She held out a pale hand. "Liebchen," she said. "Come away with me to the forest."

62 - That's Where You'll Find Me

My benefactor would issue daily missives, written onto corn husk dolls, initialled DG. I kept them in a sack and would lay them out in the evening to see whether the words formed any sort of linear narrative. As far as I could tell they were naught but garbled musings. Yet I followed where she led. Along a dusty brick road, strangled by weeds, to the sad green ruins of a once magnificent city.

There she finally revealed herself, wild eyed and grey haired from decades of isolation.

I proffered my hand. "Dorothy Gale, I presume.

63 - The Absent Father

"Have you been time travelling again, Timothy?"

"Aw, mum. How can you tell?"

"Biscuit crumbs on the quilt. You always bring back Jammie Dodgers when you go to the 1970's."

"Do you think I'll ever find him?"

"He doesn't want to be found, Timothy. He's holed up with the tart with the tie-died tee-shirt. Only your father could hook up with someone who's young enough to be his great-great grandmother."

"You miss him too, mum. Admit it."

"Miss him? Suffice to say I'll bloody swing for him if his relentless philandering causes a rift in the space time continuum."

64 - The Art of the Assassin

Vincenzo Chiara craved notoriety.

It was best not to stay upwind of him. His lumbering frame reeked like a piggery. He studiously cultured this stench. Wanted his victims to know that death was upon them when he arrived like the dark angel on their doorstep.

His favoured method of execution was to place his Luger under the chin and plaster the ceiling with brains. He said the effect was like modern art.

I was unsettled in his presence. But in the war to anoint me as kingpin of the south shore he was my shock and awe.

65 - The Box of Delights

"Do you have to inhale like that?"

"Like what?"

"The trick is to breathe through your nose."

"I can't. Sinus issues."

"Three days! Trapped in the darkness with your endless wheezing. I feel like strangling you."

"It saddens me to hear that."

"Why do you do that?"

"What?"

"Talk all pretentious like that?"

"You're in a mood. Let's try the lid again."

"You try the fucking lid again."

"You sulk in the corner and moan then."

"For Christ sake, could you just inhale properly?"

"What are you doing? Get off me!"

"Sinuses. I'll cure your fucking sinuses…"

66 - The Caution Pouch

Inside the Caution Pouch Katsumi began to sweat. Her hands hovered over the controls as she approached the anomaly. No one had been this close before. The skin of the Pouch stretched but did not tear. She saw the anomaly in all of its vast kaleidoscopic glory - jagged slithers of past present and future, swirling and colliding.

The Pouch began to tumble and drift.

She became trapped in a pulse and repeated the moment.

She became trapped in a pulse and repeated the moment.

She became trapped in a pulse.

67 - The Chances of Anything

A fuliginous cloud rolled across Surrey, coughing toxic smoke and spewing spumes of soot, swallowing entire suburbs like some poisonous beast.

Daphne was swept along in the stampede of fleeing citizens. In the dash she twisted her ankle. Worried she would be trampled underfoot she took shelter in a doorway.

A gigantic three-legged monstrosity lumbered out of the miasma, incinerating a line of blue helmeted constables. She knew this mechanical atrocity from her grandmother's tales.

1st September 1939, dawn of the second war, Chamberlain's interplanetary diplomacy failed. From the direction of Woking came the caterwauling of rusted sirens.

68 - The Confession of Sergeant Bill Gruff

I am haunted by my actions. Driven to confess.

My orders were confidential. I was a soldier. Carried them out without question. Just before midnight I would station myself down river. When the *'trolls'* emerged from under the bridges I would pluck them out of existence with bullets from a high-powered rifle. It was clinical and efficient. The top brass called it "weeding the garden of Eden".

Despite what you were led to believe Neanderthals were only very recently driven to extinction. Their demise was deliberately engineered. No place for them amongst the poison roses.

69 - The Consequence of Sticky Fingers

The Filth are after me.

I found the Eighth Gate.

Hey, I'm an opportunist thief. When I saw that big, stonking ruby I yoinked it.

Now the Trans-dimensional Felonies Division want my balls on a skillet. The ruby is a religious artefact. I've gone and caused an interspecies crisis. The residents of Gate Eight are pissed off. Giant carnivorous termites tumbling through day and night. My old Ma is livid. Turfed me out on my arse. No one wants anything to do with me or the bleedin' ruby. All I can do is stay in the shadows.

70 - The Corpse Maggot

A maggot wriggles within the putrid bullet wound on the bloated corpse. The solitary survivor. She'd watched her siblings cower as the crow came down to pluck them in his beak.

She gorges on rancid flesh. Her slow metamorphosis features fidgety legs and busy wings. Skyward she flits, dodging the beak of the swooping crow.

Time passes.

The buzzing blue fly returns to the corpse. In amnesia of the risk posed by crows she lays her eggs within the festering well of the putrid bullet wound.

Soon her offspring gorge on rancid flesh. The crow circles slowly down.

71 - The Dollmaker

Although the summer heat was oppressive we kept our windows locked. It gave us a fools' sense of security. The corn husk dolls proliferated. And on each issue a carved set of initials. Sudden invisible violence visited on the bearer. Sunrise bringing the dread of what the night may have deposited on the doorstep. The victims ostracised for fear of assault by association.

But October came. Leaves tumbled in russet swirls. No more dolls. Whatever seized our town had departed for warmer climes. The wind sighed in proxy of our relief as we tended our lesions and wounds.

72 - The Farm Hand

On fields as wide as infinite oceans an armada of mechanised harvesters was bringing in the grain. Hernandez watched from the lilting shanty as they moved in a synchronised column toward a rust blood horizon where sheaths of barley touched alien sky.

To the east gargantuan silos strained at the seams.

Hernandez ran the diagnostic software to check for any mechanical faults. Across the galaxy there was an ignorance of the power he wielded. The push of a button might plunge entire worlds into starvation.

Smiling he sent his proposal for a substantial uplift in pay

73 - The Hunting of Utopia

The first day of simulated spring and the air from the vents was pleasantly ambient. Jacques and Gill strolled the wide corridor of Main Street. Synthetic blossoms floated in the air. Little mechanical wild birds chirruped gaily in the girders. At the atrium their fellow band members were assembling around the replica of Michelangelo's statue of David.

Gill twirled her baton. "This is going to be the best Easter Parade ever."

"Not a meteor storm in sight," agreed Jacques.

Cloaked in darkness the alien stealth cruiser pursued the starship's heat signature with the relentless persistence of a bloodhound.

74 - The Last Noel?

The chicken was leathery. The sage in the stuffing like chopped up twigs.

"How do you know it's even Christmas?" asked Beth.

Tom nodded to where the ash fall had blanketed the countryside in swirling grey drifts.

"Good a day as any, I'd say."

He handed her a piece of fused glass he'd found.

"Got you a gift."

The wind gusted and tinkled the chimes they'd hung for protection.

"Jingle Bells?" said Tom.

"Coincidence," said Beth, gnawing on a wing. Her radiation sores were weeping again.

He hung a cracked bauble on his pathetic tree.

75 - The Liberty of Statues

A pride of stone lions basked in the wedge of sunlight that spread across Trafalgar Square, beyond them a gaggle of mossy gargoyles, claws clacking. Statues had been animated by anomalous quirk.

Nelson rose gigantically to address the assembly. Several Churchills, a Mandela and a Mountbatten, children of the kinder transport, Boadicea in her chariot, a winged airman, generals and knights.

Nelson's voice was like the grinding of gravel, but his words spoke a simple truth.

"Stone is solid – flesh is soft."

The statues rumbled a thunderous appreciation.

A fragile human was crushed to prove the point.

76 - The Librarian

The serial killer known as the *Librarian* had struck again.

This time, along with the severed digits, he left a first edition of Nabokov's Lolita. As usual there was no corpse. The victim was identified by his fingerprints as Anthony Vermont, recently found not guilty of forcefully seducing young girls with the aid of Rohypnol.

The detective assigned to the case furtively devoured the remains of the evidence and wiped blood from his lips as he selected a novel from his extensive collection, appropriate to the crimes of his next intended victim.

77 - The Miner Forty-Niner

My Darling Clementine,
This video message bears witness to my dreadful sorrow.

Out on asteroid belt 49 we are perched on the edge of oblivion. The Interstellar Mining Corporation went into liquidation, leaving us stranded. We ran out of PPE. The synthetic membranes which protect us from the ravages of gamma rays are shedding like snake skin. Soon we will be plagued by aggressive melanomas.

The minerals we have harvested are too precious to abandon. They will be retrieved eventually. But sadly we are dead men walking.

Watch the stars. Think of me.
All my love
Rocket Man

78 - The Model T

"This year's model has a fairy friendly grill," said the salesman.

"Golly gee," said Smith. "Such innovation."

"Mr Ford is determined that the 1930's will be an era of harmony with our tiny cousins," said the salesman.

"And she'll take me to the end of the rainbow on a full tank?" asked Smith.

"There and back," said the salesman. "There's even a compartment in the trunk for the pot of gold."

"Shucks," said Smith. "Fill up that fountain pen with my blood. I'll have my soul signed away in a jiffy."

79 - The Next Temptation

The cosmonauts stepped cautiously though the hushed ruins of the dead city. Claws of yellow vines smothering bizarrely angled tilts of architecture. Centuries of salt deposits crunching underfoot.

The coordinates suggested they had found Visisirin, cradle of Hashemian civilisation. If legends were to believed they might also find the hidden vaults containing poetic stanzas with the apparent power to tear the very fabric of reality on a single recital.

Bushkov turned to Zuravleva and spoke through his comms. "How do you feel?"

Her reply caused a cold shiver to pass through him. "Like Eve about to seize the apple."

80 - The Plan to End Austerity

"As a consequence of budget restraints," explained the Minister, "we have decided to scrap the project."

"What about the prisoner?' asked Harkness. "There's a backlog of tests to conduct. The stigmata still bleed thirty years on."

The Minister shuffled papers. "He's a burden we can ill afford. Bids from several foreign governments mean a windfall for the Treasury."

Harkness sighed. "We sell him for 30 pieces of silver?"

The Minister drummed his fingers. "If he actually is the Messiah you'd have proved it by now."

Harkness shook his head. "Thus spake Thomas."

81 - The Riot Started in Cell Block Number Four

While excavating the ruins of an office block Hester discovered a box of paper clips. She concealed them on her person and managed to evade being selected by the guards for a random search. That night clips were passed from cell to cell and used to pick the locks. The entire population of the prison reached the room where their husbands were suspended in huge specimen jars. By sunrise the corridors ran scarlet with the blood of the invaders. By noon the insurrection was quelled. But now they knew what was possible. Next time it would be different.

82 - The Staff

I inherited the staff with my uncle's grotesquely baroque hotel.

They had the unsettling air of some wan faced, incestuous clan. Their sullen indifference tested me to the limit. They'd scuttle like roaches to their quarters, whispering conspiracies.

I vegetated in the conservatory, sipping anaemic tea from cracked china, pondering the solitary guest who never ventured from his room.

The chef sharpened his cleaver. The housekeeper folded yards of linen. The gardener constructed a pyre. The old clock in the foyer ticked its monotonous tock. As autumn bled slowly into winter, death stared back at me from tainted mirrors.

83 - The Ties That Bind

His bed shook like a raft on a turbulent river.

A voice screeched. "Jason, what do you want in your sandwich?"

He groaned. "Violet! Could you please just stop?"

The room echoed to her reply. "I am your mother. Don't you dare call me Violet!"

He sat up and stared into the gloom.

"You died twenty years ago. Let me go. You've destroyed every relationship I ever had."

Invisible hands yanked open the curtains.

"Get up! You'll be late!"

The apron strings tightened like a noose around his neck.

"I hate you," he spat.

The disembodied slap sent him reeling.

84 - The Tramp Who Fell To Earth

The tramp looked up them, eyes too big for his head. He began decanting tarry strings of tobacco.

"Tell us again about the invasion?"

PC Singh nudged PC Henderson.

The tramp rolled a Rizla.

"Swore I'd devote my life to it. Been here since 1955."

"Guess they're not coming." Henderson winked.

"Guess I will need to act on my own volition."

The tramp's eyelids slid vertically over bulbous eyes.

PC Singh jumped back.

"Bloody hell!"

The tramp moved with startling speed.

"Two down," he said, coldly stepping over their eviscerated bodies. "Seven and a half billion to go."

85 - The Unexpected Cinema

Remember that night in Bucharest?

The old town. A labyrinth of narrow streets. The unexpected cinema. Like a temple from antiquity. Blue carpets. Red wallpaper. Ornate angels in the alcoves.

Perfume from a bygone year tainting the air with sour ferment. The flicker of the screen. Monochrome figures performing in grainy silence. Hunched within shadows a piano player. His bone white fingers caressing bone white ivory.

Ghosts to the left and to the right.

Though we fled, the rawest part of us remained. Bathed in the glow of the ectoplasmic projector our souls anticipated credits that never rolled.

86 - The War of the Farmlands

This was anything but *quaint*. Milk *maids* all a row. Quite contrary. No intention of looking pretty. Armed with steel rimmed milk pails. Only the clatter of cloven hooves on the cobbled yard broke the silent tension.

The boy blue blew on his horn.

The maids advanced in columns across the turnip fields. Their arms spun like windmills. The pails howled like banshees. Stunning blows scattered teeth to the dirt like fallen pearls.

The enemy tumbled down with bloodied crowns. The cattle came tumbling after. Tramping corpses to the dirt. No one could put them together again.

87 - The Water, Like a Witch's Oils

We drifted sluggishly into still waters. The ominous moan of the wind like the mournful dirge of the drowned. A one eyed crewman fingered the frets on his Spanish guitar. He claimed his plectrum was the frozen tear of a mermaid. It may simply have been sea-glass.

The captain tapped out his pipe. "You regret your decision to seek passage aboard the Anchor of Anubis?"

"Not at all," I lied.

Something grotesque surfaced momentarily on the swell. I blinked it was gone. The captain reached calmly for his harpoon gun. Dread seized my bones.

88 - This Explains Everything

Twenty years ago I served as First Mate on a merchant vessel.

Early on the first day of the new millennium we docked in Zanzibar.

Drunk on half my wages I found myself in a squalid flea market. An antiques trader sold me a lamp he swore had once belonged to Aladdin. It should have been something to laugh about when I sobered up.

But it was an act of global terrorism. The Genie I released set out to destroy civilisation. 9/11, ISIS, Trump, Brexit, Covid, it's all down to my stupid and reckless, booze fuelled shenanigans.

89 - Time, in Quaaludes and Red Wine

It's discombobulating to give a eulogy for one who simultaneously died last week - and 62 years ago. Some scurrilously decry him for being so erudite, yet squandering the potential of his Hallucinogenic Engine.

Friends, he didn't meander aimlessly through time. His visits to 1950's Lubbock, Texas had purpose. Buddy Holly was the subject of an audacious experiment. Might altering a single event alter history itself? Lucky he boarded that flight, you say? Saved from the ripple of butterfly wings.

But are we sure of that?

Perhaps our present is no longer the future it once was in his past?

90 - To See a Fine Lady

London was rotting to mulch beneath a rustling emerald canopy. Serpentine ivy and rambling root tubers cowling skyscrapers and smothering streets, while deep within the veins of these verdant depths seared fragments of the seed bombs bled to rust.

The loop was the only clear route. Adil circumnavigated its blister inducing circumference with a dogged determination, proclaiming the prophecy at every settlement.

Finally, he settled by a forest of thistles to await the arrival of the fine lady. Slugs on her fingers, grubs on her toes, blighting the weeds wherever she goes.

91 - Ticks and Crosses

When they could not *wean* us from our addictions, they deposited us in a walled town depopulated for the purpose. Our foreheads were marked in *indelible* ink. Some with a green tick. Some with a black cross.

These marks fired our paranoia. What did they symbolise? How were we categorised?

The manual they left for us held no clues. Pages of *extraneous* text with no apparent purpose.

We split into tribes. Ticks on the hill. Crosses in the hollow.

Now we plot war and wish genocide on those who carry the wrong mark.

Was this the intent?

92 - To Kill a Manticore

The knight was perched on a log by the fire. Although his armour had been burnished, the dents and creases were visibly obvious. His hands shook. His face was wrinkled and scarred.

"*You* killed the Wyvern?" asked Christabel.

"Forty odd years ago," sighed the knight. His breath reeked of fermented ale. His condition worsened, armour rattling to his palsied trembles.

"There's a manticore on the rampage," said Christabel. "We need a champion."

The knight clattered to his feet and struck an awkward pose. "I'm your man."

Christabel groaned. This wasn't going to end well.

93 - Upgrades

Dan began to *bristle* when he saw his neighbour clattering along the street in his new exoskeleton.

O'Mara grinned at him over tungsten teeth, fibre-optic eyes gleaming smugly.

"Like my new upgrade?" he asked. "Courtesy of the NHS. You should get an adaption. You're over 65. You're *eligible*."

"Over my dead body," snapped Dan.

O'Mara showed off the pneumatic sheathes that fit his arthritic finger like a glove.

"I'll be laying bricks into my eighties while you scrimp and scrape on your pension."

Seething, Dan turned and walked away, a martyr to his aches and pains and ailments.

94 - Underworld Endorsement

Dude, this guy is spooky. He's got alchemy in his fingertips.

Get him a key. An old key. An unwanted key. A key that's caked in rust. Then give him something to lubricate it. Engine oil. Baby oil. Cooking oil. He can lever any lock. Yale, Chubb, whatever. When he flicks his wrist it's like magic. Bam! The door opens, and he's in like Flynn.

Then the weirdness really kicks off. He holds out his hands, spreads his palms and swag just flies into them, like he's got magnets under his flesh.

You want a thief? He's your man.

95 - Visions of an Inferno to Come

His father's water buffalo strained in bovine muscularity against the yoke. Minh felt a thrill run through him as the cart, replete with sacks of rice, juddered forward. The buffalo lumbered along the dirt track that bounded the rice paddies.

Clouds swirled wispy hieroglyphics against the blue canvass of the sky. A mosquito buzzed his ear. The tails of the buffalo swished lazily against the flies.

Then came the nightmare vision. A premonition of forests engulfed in gargantuan balls of fire. Blistering flesh. Screams of excruciating agony. And Napalm, that dreadful foreign word, etched in hellish flames inside his head.

96 - Voice of the Orphan

Torturer General gently set the stylus to the grooves of the record. The song was beautiful. It lifted his mood. The accursed orphan had once sung like this to rouse the masses. Now its ravaged tongue hung dripping on a hook, blood crusting on its cherubim chin.

As the music rose to a crescendo he circled the child like a wolf closing on a lamb. Without warning it leapt at him and sank its filthy little teeth into the flesh of his arm.

He howled holy hell.

He'd stolen its voice - but it had other weapons!

97 - Watching Me – Watching You – Watching Me

"This is the scene where you are watching a film which shows you watching a film which shows you getting killed while you are watching a film which shows you getting killed," said the director.

"And I get killed while watching it?" asked the actor.

The director nodded.

"It's the defining moment of film. Life imitating art imitating life."

"What's my motivation?" asked the actor.

"Make your imitation of life imitating art as lifelike and artistic as possible."

On the set the film played out. At the point when the actor was watching himself get whacked on the head with a cricket bat while watching himself get whacked on the head with a cricket bat he was whacked on the head with a cricket bat.

Blood splattered the lens.

"That was a load of rubbish," said yet another version of the actor.

And was promptly whacked on the head.

98 - Whiskey Galore (The Kraken's Plot)

The Kraken knew what motivated the Scots. When the hull of the merchant vessel passed over she followed to the coastal waters of the Outer Hebrides. There she struck like lightning, shattering the ship from aft to stern.

Seeing barrels of whiskey bobbing on the brine was enough to provoke the islanders into a frenzy.

The Kraken lay in the shallows, patiently biding her time. Soon the beach was like Sauchiehall Street on a Saturday night. And when they were suitably stewed and pickled she plucked them with her multiple tentacles and popped them into her salivating maw.

99 - White Cat – White Heat

He'd kept a low profile for over fifty years.

Back in the heady era of the white heat of technology, there had been generous public funds and little government interference.

As a consequence he may have successfully sent a small white kitten hurtling into the future. But the Philistines came. Projects shelved, machinery dismantled. His reports archived, subject to the Official Secrets Act.

He waits on Hampstead Heath. Weary old heart slowly sinking. Time ticks by. He sighs in acceptance of his failure. As he turns to leave a joyous sound seems to fill the entire universe.

"Meow."

100 - Wulvensong

From the forest a portentous scintilla of wulvensong, attempting to howl down the moon.

Inside the hunting lodge the sisters of the Riding Hood broke their communion bread and shared it out. A third each. The blessed red garment was laid out on the table. Sinead bent to kiss it, then scattered six silver bullets across the crimson silk.

Roisin turned pale. "Sure, is that all we have left?"

Sinead nodded solemnly.

"Jesus, Mary and Joseph," intoned Deirdre, hurriedly making the sign of the cross.

The flames in the hearth stuttered.

The howling drew nearer.

Part Two - Four Serials

Husang

Husang - Part One (Atlantic Crossing)

Her father's recital of the poem was interrupted by the predatory circling of a land shark.

Husang shot it through the head with her harpoon. Moving swiftly, they removed the spear, wiped it clean, tumbled the gleaming black body into the back of the wagon.

Back on the jockey board Hu San yanked the reins. Their lobster heaved against its harness and began its ponderous descent into the canyon.

"Keep within the wheel ruts," cautioned her father.

Husang nodded.

Her father cleared his throat.

"It is an Ancient mariner," he intoned.

Husang - Part Two (Husang and the Land Whale)

Husang teetered on the pedestal, shovelling great squirming heaps of worms into the yawning orifice of the land whale.

He moaned in delight. The ground trembled, almost toppling the pedestal. He had trebled in size. His grey hide was speckled in green moss and black lichen.

Husang turned to her father, unsettled by the whole affair.

"If he gets any bigger he might try to eat me."

"He won't turn on his provider little one," assured her father, fetching a new barrel of worms. "But when he is fully grown he will surely devour our enemies."

112

Husang – Part Three (The Artefact)

While Husang was gathering specimens in one of the rock pools she found a small, rusted thing amongst the sediment. By the time she had brought it to her grandfather the sky had turned crimson. "Paperclip," he sighed, holding the object on the leathery palm of his hand. "I knew these as a boy." A tear of nostalgia ran down the crags of his cheeks.

Husang whispered this new word.

"Paperclip."

The shape of its mystery of it felt invigorating on her lips.

The land whale began to bellow, hungry to be fed.

Extinction Trilogy

Extinction Trilogy 1 - Avian-Sapiens

The Proctor was displaying full male mating plumage. Feathers curling like erotic fronds of fern.

Veshula quelled her fiery arousal.

"You can vouch for their authenticity?" he asked, beady eyes scrutinising the pale bones she had laid out before him.

"The onus was on me to prove the existence of intelligent simian society."

The proctor stroked his serrated beak. "You theorise that they regressed as we evolved?"

Veshula jutted her downy neck in agreement.

"Female folly," cawed the Proctor, clawing the bones violently from the table. "Destroy them."

Veshula genuflected, soon she'd reveal the thousands she'd uncovered in the Flatlands.

Extinction Trilogy 2 - The Theory of Giants

There was an earring buried in the loamy soil beneath the forest of wild spearmint that had colonised the ancient park. Drone dug it up. Hauled it to the mound. Set it before his pink, bloated Queen. Transmitted his thoughts

'Proof of intelligent life before *us*?'

The Queen rippled grotesquely.

'What is the word of God?'

Drone bowed his antennae in deference.

'That She created Termites in Her own image.'

'The artefact is heresy,' transmitted the Queen. 'Have it destroyed.'

Drone backed away, dragging the earring. Contemplating science over superstition. Fomenting rebellion. Conceiving the theory of giants.

Extinction Trilogy 3 - The Meek Shall Inherit

The orchids were bountiful. Their scent perfumed the air. They colonised the marshy canyon beds which had once been the mighty Atlantic and spread in vast legions across the moss covered hummocks of fallen cities.

Dorsal sepals the texture of flowing satin would vibrate to sing of mythical bipeds. While the allure of their seductive labellum stupefied bees and caused them to hum in harmony.

At night an eerie ambition would stretch their stems skyward. In audible sigh they would indulge in the unified dream that one day they might boldly go to seed the stars.

Dawn of the Amsterdamned

Dawn of the Amsterdamned (Part One)

Our protective barricade of bicycles and breeze blocks encircles the bridges and banks. Dams built from upturned barges stem the canal, causing the water to recede. We are an odd bunch. Prostitutes, punks and policemen. Crouched on pallets. Caked in mud. A tragedy unfolding.

The peacock we rescued becomes vexed on the approach of walking cadavers. We are low on ammunition. We wait till the juddering creatures become entangled in the bicycle frames before taking them out.

Automatic gunfire echoes in the vicinity of the port. We scan the skies, clinging to the hope of incoming helicopters.

Dawn of the Amsterdamned (Part Two)

We escaped Amsterdam in a tourist bus. Eighteen of us. There was a CD in the CD player. Sweetheart of the Rodeo. We listened, sharing out the last of the stroopwaffles. After much procrastination we headed north for Groningen.

To the side of the road evidence of resistance. Three cadavers lashed to the sails of a windmill, eerily revolving.

Our tally of weapons was dire. The dial on the petrol gage dropped lower. Gram Parsons sang of tall pines in North Carolina. In the pink acres of the tulip fields herds of festering corpses assembled.

Dawn of the Amsterdamned (Part Three)

We took refuge inside di Bijenkorf Department store. Our number dwindled to eleven. One of the policemen nursing a

116

fractured collar bone. Garlands of pot-pourri around our necks to disguise the stench of putrefying flesh that fouled the air.

Someone was reading aloud from a novel by Charles De Lint.

We had no escape. German tanks patrolled the border. The walls trembled to another explosion. NATO had ordered the blanket bombing of the cemeteries. Collateral casualties considered a price worth paying. The living, by default, defecting to the burgeoning army of the dead.

Dawn of the Amsterdamned (Part Four)

Six of us escaped the overwhelming of the department store.

We linked up with another group, crammed into the back of a delivery truck. A bearded Imam endlessly fingered his worry beads next to someone we couldn't help but stare at. A living legend. Barry Hay from Golden Earring.

The message on the radio was to head for the evacuation zone at the Port of Rotterdam. The truck swerved to avoid a wall of rabid cadavers. Barry strummed his blood splattered guitar. His voice instilling hope. "Been drivin' all night. Hands wet on the wheel."

The Outlaw

The Outlaw – Episode One – He Casts No Shadow

The outlaw percolates cactus juice to make peyote gin. A potent concoction. He sips it. Claims he is rendered invisible to his enemies.

This may be true. Once I saw him shoot a Pinkerton detective in the head. No one so much as blinked at his presence.

I dress him. Like his pageboy from some romance of yore.

Satin shirt and boots that gleam. Silver spurs on his heels and silver buckles on his belts. His Stetson hangs low above his eyes. When he steps out into the midday sun he casts no shadow in his wake.

The Outlaw – Episode Two – This Is How He Owns Us

In the flicker of the campfire we exchanged tales of how we first encountered the Outlaw.

"Camptown racecourse," said O'Brien. "With the cast of a travelling review. I had bad gambling debts. Men came to fix me, armed with razors. He appeared like a swirling wraith. Silver spurs and silver buckles. Hauled me away by the shirt collar. Next thing I know I'm in Kansas."

I touched the rope scar on my neck, recalling how he snatched me from the noose.

"Rode with him ever since," said O'Brian.

"This is how he owns us," whispered Three Crows.

The Outlaw – Episode Three - The Silencing of the Crickets

O'Brien called his Winchester the *maiden*. She was always on his arm. She'd shattered the deadlock on the front door of many a bank. Now he held her tensely to his shoulder, watching for signs the darkness.

The horses snorted and kicked their hooves when the Outlaw unfurled like a wraith from the church. Three Crows a step behind, eyes raw from her tears.

"Where to now?" I asked.

"Shenandoah.

The Outlaw's uncanny voice silenced the chirruping crickets.

The anomalous hush made me shiver.

"We'll intercept Coyote there."

Each word he uttered felt like an incantation.

The Outlaw – Episode Four - The Road to Shenandoah

The Outlaw wasn't evil and the law wasn't good. Not that simple.

We joked a lot as we rode toward Shenandoah. A distraction from the flies. O'Brien would recite vulgar rhymes from his music hall days. Claimed they were allegories for weightier matters.

Trust me they were not.

"You shouldn't ought to say stuff like that in front of a lady," Three Crows Cawing would taunt.

We'd wink. "I'll write one about you."

The Outlaw would mumble beneath his Stetson. "That would be a bad move, partner."

Me and Three Crows would laugh at O'Brien's nervousness.

The Outlaw – Episode Five - South of the Border, Down Mexico Way

The cantina in the little border town was so crammed with Pinkertons and Rangers its rooftop was sweating at the eaves. Extravagantly moustachioed men swaggered and boasted with delusional zeal that the Outlaw would soon be jerking on the end of a hangman's rope.

Coyote prowled the puddles of liquor, shifting shapes within the cloying tobacco fug, gleefully malevolent in his itch for mischief.

They were welcome to the Outlaw. It was Kiowa woman he coveted. His claws were sharp enough to slice her flesh like butter. The bundle she bore in her belly would soon be his.

The Outlaw – Episode Six - Swampland Blues

We chose the wrong fork in the road.

Our horses became stuck in the quagmire. They struggled to exhaustion. We shot them out of mercy, followed the Outlaw on our bellies, dragging Three Crows Cawing on her back. Her unborn child kicked up holy hell in her swollen belly.

She gave birth beneath the vines and creepers. Like her father the child cast no shadow.

We heard Coyote howling as he circled in. Three Crows hugged her baby. O'Brien shouldered his Winchester. The Outlaw loaded his six guns with silver bullets.

The Outlaw – Episode Seven - Eighteen with a Bullet

The doctor reeked of whisky. He touched the belt strapped around my thigh.

"If I undo that buckle he'll bleed like a sow."

"Call yourself a medical man?" railed O'Brien. "You couldn't diagnose a wart on the end of my dick!"

"My father was a parish surgeon," came the pompous reply.

"And you're jack shit," O'Brien snapped back.

The bullet had shattered my knee. Fever brought visions of myself as a peg-legged cripple, begging in the dirt.

Three Crows stroked my brow.

"The Outlaw will work his magics."

Soon, I hoped.

The edges of the room grew hazy.

The Outlaw - Episode Eight -Daddy's Home

Three Crows cowered within the cloister.

There was no valid reason to flee to this dreadful place. She had sobbed here as a child, nursing purple bruises. The pious nuns wanted to beat the Christianity into her. It simply drove her into the clutches of a whorehouse mistress.

A slither of sound made her draw tremulous breath.

Coyote?

She hushed her heart and dared a fearful peek.

It was the Outlaw, eyes gleaming beneath the brim of his Stetson, shadowless in the flicker of the altar candles.

Three Crows whispered to her unborn child.

"He came for us."

The Outlaw – Episode Nine- The Debt Collector

He took her so fast the doorknob was still in her hand. Three Crows wondered if it might be used as a weapon. "Where are we?"

Coyote grinned over jagged teeth.

"The *dreaming* between worlds. Your friends can't help you."

He ran his leathery paw over her swell.

"When your child is delivered I will be its guardian."

"The hell you will."

Coyote cast a yellow eyed glare.

"The Outlaw owes me. I gave him his guns. His firstborn is rightfully mine."

He pressed his pointed little ear to her belly, growling as he listened for a heartbeat.

The Outlaw – Episode Ten - The Last Chance Saloon

The Outlaw lurked within the gloomy ruins of the ancient saloon. Jagged moth trails etched his Stetson, gossamer spider web draped from the brim to his shoulder. Roaches danced like pets on his lap. By some miracle his breath still rattled.

He recalled me in a befuddled manner.

"Fifty years gone a drunken doctor cauterised your shattered knee."

I cranked up the gramophone and sat before him. He placed his hand on my head like a father. As Tosca played we cried for O'Brien and Three Crows - and a little boy stolen by a bad prairie dog.

www.ingramcontent.com/pod-product-compliance
Lightning Source LLC
Chambersburg PA
CBHW021153210626
46807CB00019B/3247